My days in London

Mehraveh Firouz

F
×
M

© Firouz Media 2022
All rights reserved

All rights reserved by the publisher. No parts of this publication may be reproduced, stored in a retrieval system, or transmitted in any form or by any means, electronic, mechanical, photocopying, recording, or otherwise, without the prior permission of the publisher.

ISBN: 978-1-7396603-0-7

Firouz Media
www.firouzmedia.com
contact@firouzmedia.com
IG: @firouzmedia

Author:
Mehraveh Firouz
Illustrator:
Shirin MalekEsmaili
Cover Designer:
Sina Rouh

Author's note:

The Persian language is commonly considered a genderless language. Since I wrote this story initially in Farsi, the genderless pronouns came naturally to me and I decided not to reveal the main character (i.e. the peddler) or their former lover's gender. Even though I call their former lover Feri, this name is considered a shortened name or nickname for both girls and boys in Iran.

Stacey Williams, my amazing editor, and I decided to go genderless in the English translation of the book to reflect the original text. However, we are aware that using they-them-their is an active choice. We would be choosing our characters to be non-binary which puts a different contextual slant on the story that isn't mentioned elsewhere. But maybe that's how we should tell a story of migration… Genderless!

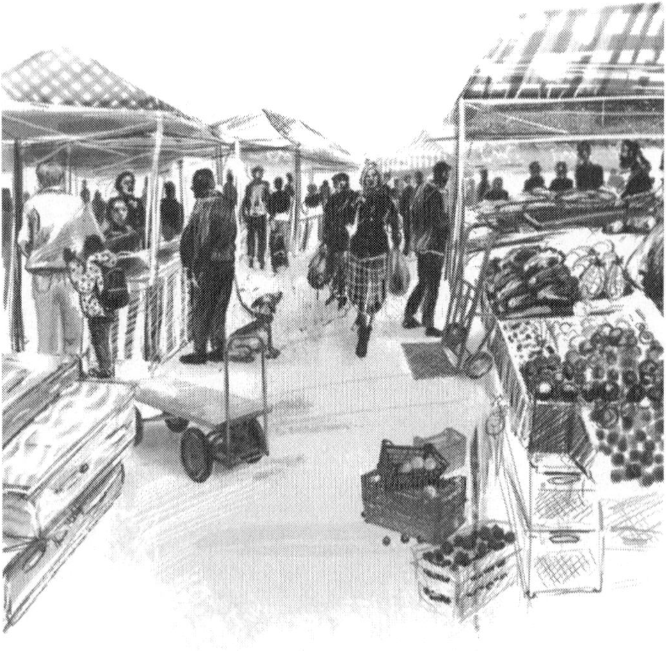

"How did I get all the way to London, only to end up selling Italian pastries and Greek olives?" I say.
A plump middle-aged woman smiled and says "what's the problem with that?"
"Isn't it random?", I say.
Never thought I'd end up like this…A street vendor!
Her voice echoes in my ears, "what's the problem with that?"
Her voice is replaced by my mum's: "Thank God…. at least you're working for yourself. No boss telling you what to do, or what not to do".
Why do we all want everything to be perfect?
Bored, my internal antagonist asks:
What do you mean WE?

I had no idea it was so proud!
"How about our Italian Pastries?" I say to a man walking by my stall.
I see his white teeth and his steps speeding up.
"No thanks!" he says, smiling.
Maybe if I'd not dropped out of Uni, and got my History BA, I'd know why we want to be the boss, with all the responsibilities and burdens.
"Look! Leo's eating the dog food!" laughs Clanzy, an elderly Jamaican man, who sells shoes and clothes at the stall next to mine.
I stare at Leo wearing an army uniform
"Why not? I had a fifty pound bet on it…
Could I have one of your tomatoes to get rid of the taste?
We bet five pounds per spoonful, and I ate ten."
Chewing on tomatoes, he went over to his ladies' clothes stall.
There were no customers, so I left the stall for a smoke.
Usually, when I want to smoke, I stand by the Ali's fruit stall, opposite Clanzy's stall.
That way I can see if I've got any customers, and also chat to Ali.
He's a nice little Bangladeshi man…I wondered why his boxes of fruit and veg were so empty today.
In his funny accent, with a twinkle in his eye, he said, "This is my last day at the market.

Tomorrow I'm going on holiday for two weeks!"

Where to? I asked excitedly.

"Saudi Arabia".

"So you're going to Mecca! Cool, I love going there too."

"No, I've done the Big One already. I'm just visiting this time."

I realise he means Umrah…

I think to myself it's a good job it's me who's asking him. If he had to explain to an English person, it would be a bit like the story of the big room and the small room where I lived as a kid…

I take one last deep inhale before putting out my half-smoked cigarette.

A girl who could be Polish is looking for me at my stand; I can tell a Polish girl by the colour of her eyes, a particular shade between green and blue.

"Uh, why weren't you here yesterday?"

"Excuse me…" I laugh.

I mean it in the sarcastic Iranian sense, meaning - it's my own business.

Unfortunately, she didn't get my meaning.

I was very lazy and sleepy, I say.

This was the third time she'd come to buy garlic.

It's a kind of pickled garlic mixed with crushed paprika and olive oil, a beautiful orange colour, but surely tastes and smells far too garlicky for a lady with those blue-green eyes!

"Wow! This garlic is so nice, I'll have a big bowl", she says.

"Where are you from?"

"I'm a hybrid. On one side I'm Swedish, from Gutenberg, and on the other side I'm Polish". I greet her by saying Shema, which means hello in Polish. "Gutenberg, I was there one time, It's really beautiful!"

"Yes, really. And it's much cleaner than London".

As I was weighing the girl's order, she said "Today is my day off, too. I'm going home...so, cool that I have lots of garlic!"

"What about your partner? Do they like garlic too?!" I asked

I don't normally ask personal questions; The answers won't matter to me! And I'm not a prying nosy Rosy! But I do think sometimes this curiosity is part of customer service. Demonstrating good manners and a connection; yet the fact is, I don't really know how to interact with others properly, and it comes over as impertinence!

"No, I'm single now. I was engaged with a foolish boy for eight months, we met at work..." And of course, she won't stop there, making me wish I hadn't ferret in her personal life...

"You bought your garlic so it's time to go!", I'm thinking.

She mentioned something about investment banking. I assumed she worked somewhere in the city, but it's impossible!

She can't have a job like that with such basic command of English. Not that my English is any good! But I certainly shy away from filling in a form for an office job…! Maybe I'm underestimating myself, or I have expectations that are too high about speaking correctly…I guess I just don't want to apply and humiliate myself for no reason.

"Where do you live?" she asks.

I don't like to say; but hey, she's a regular.

"North London", I say.

I'm not going to get rid of her until I get a wrinkled fiver out of her…

A boy who'd already bought sweets this morning is back standing next to them.

I put sweets and biscuits on the left half of my table, and the olive buckets on the other side.

This boy is standing by the left side, next to the pastries

Normally, I find it a challenge to recognize faces.

For instance, if someone buys something from me, leaves my stand and then comes back, I would never remember their face.

I realized it when an old man said "how can you not remember this face?!" He was right. No one could forget that face, it was a little scary.

I'm not here to explain to people that their money pays for my rent and bills; I just give them the best quality pastries and olives, in exchange for cash. That's it. Period, next line…

So it's strange that I remember the boy in front of me now.

Earlier today he'd got one of these Italian cannoli, the ones filled with a green cream that is pure pistachio, but looks artificial next to the vanilla or chocolate creams.

It wasn't his face I remembered, but his t-shirt…

If I can come and work every day until I've got enough to pay the bills for the next two weeks, I'll go and buy clothes. I have just three sets of clothes. I change them every two days, and I wash them all at the weekend.

"These are the best cannoli I've had in my entire life. Can I get two more? In two separate bags?"

Of course, I said.

"Here you are, have a nice day."

I crane my neck to see Clanzy.

"Hey, Clanzy, shall we have some tea?"

A while ago, he started bringing an electric kettle to boil water.

He usually makes tea twice a day, once in the morning when we're setting up the stall, and once again while we're packing up.

I offer him some sweets. He likes the coconut macaroon. In his own words, it tastes of his home country, Jamaica.

Before Clanzy's electric kettle arrangement, we used to get our tea from a nearby café.

It was sixty pence with a market trader's discount.

I often multiply the days, weeks, months and years to see how much money I'm handing over to someone; so two cups of tea, twice a day, multiplied by weeks, months, years…. That's how much I'm paying the café owner.

It's a café where any time of day you can order breakfast, as its name makes it clear: "All day breakfast".
But the Turkish owner put Iskender kebab and stuffed aubergine on the menu. Whenever his wife comes over, she tastes one of my green Italian olives. I rarely go there because I'm tired of explaining to his mother that I want a cappuccino, so froth the milk please! Don't boil it! I even went behind the coffee machine, and showed her how to put the steel jug under the steam tube till it foams... but to no avail...

"Is it ok now?" she says.

I think to myself if it wasn't for the little math that I do for summing up coffee times days times weeks times months...I'd probably rather paying two pounds and seventy pence and get my coffee on the French café at the corner, the shop which showcases its bread proudly!

But rather than stop multiplying and dividing, I drink my coffee at home in the morning, get to work, and wait for Clanzy to bring tea two hours later.

***

I usually marinate olives on Thursdays to get them ready for the weekends. Saturdays and Sundays are my wheel of fortune...I mix the pitted mammoth olives with pickled cucumbers, dried basil, garlic and colourful Spanish mushrooms.

Orange mushrooms with pitted Kalamata olives. Another bucket to mix the big green pitted olives with harissa chili sauce, garlic, pitted Kalamata and paprika powder. Then I mix small pitted olives with chopped Feta, dried parsley, pomegranate and Olive oil.

This process takes more than three hours, and if a customer comes in the meantime, I'll serve them. I can hear the hum of chat between Peter the florist and Clanzy, and another man who I believe is Indian.

Clanzy is laughing and the Indian man is nodding his head.

The Indian man passes by my stall, shaking his head in disapproval.

"Did you hear that?"

"What do you mean?" I asked.

"Do you know Leo?"

I know what he wants to say, and what the hum was about!

"Yes, so what?"

"They say he ate dog-shit this morning."

I think all people who spread rumors in the world are the same!

"Oh, no! He ate dog food for a fifty pounds bet", I clarified.

"So why are they saying Leo ate dogs shit? Eating dog food isn't weird!"

"I agree. Actually, when it's made in the factory, there are people who taste it for quality!"

The Indian man reluctantly looks at the mobile being passed between Clanzy and Peter's customers, all looking at Leo eating dog food.

* * *

I started to read the newspaper, but I sense someone coming towards me. I turn my head, and see the girl with the blue-green eyes is back again.

"I came to get two pounds of your green olives, the

very bright ones."
She points to the Sicilian olives which are soaking only in water and salt, they're fresh and juicy.
"Do you mean two pounds in money?!" I ask.
I weigh them on the scales.
"A little more."
"Four pounds? Is that enough?"
"Yes, it is."
I put the Nocellara Olive container in a bag and hand it over to her. I really want her to leave, but notice she's put her umbrella on the corner of the table...

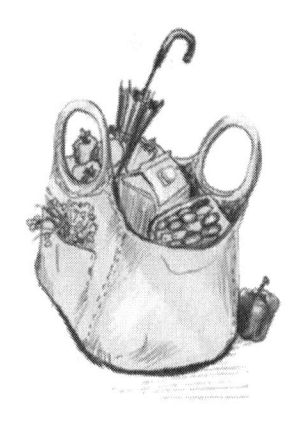

"I'm really mad today", she says.

"What happened?"

"I let one of my rooms to a boy, and the only thing I asked of him was that if he wants a cigarette, he has to go out of the house…Today I smelled smoke! And you know, the smell of cigarettes doesn't come out easily, I've only just painted the walls.

She starts to look round while she talks.

"Well, talk to him, tell him you know he's smoking inside and that you're upset and he mustn't do it again."

It was as if she never heard me.

"Maybe I should tell him to leave my house."

"But it's such a hassle to find a new lodger!" I said.

She snaps back: "Oh no. It is very easy. I have a lovely house, in a nice area. I can easily replace him with someone else".

Again I tried to explain why she should talk to him, but really I just wanted her to go away.

"Ok, I think I should listen to you and have a word with him."

If she were Iranian, and if I was more in the mood, I would have laughed out loud. I would say at last you can see some sense.

I asked her about work to change the subject. She said that her job is too complicated, requires great concentration and also that she works so hard…but I can't believe that.

"I must go, but I'll come back for these Crete Olive oils tomorrow", she says.

I'm thinking why doesn't she buy it now?

As she leaves, Clanzy comes over with a naughty look in his eyes, laughing. "Someone fancies you! Did she say she's coming back tomorrow?"

"No way! What do you mean, fancy?! She's just my customer."

"What a juicy mango!"

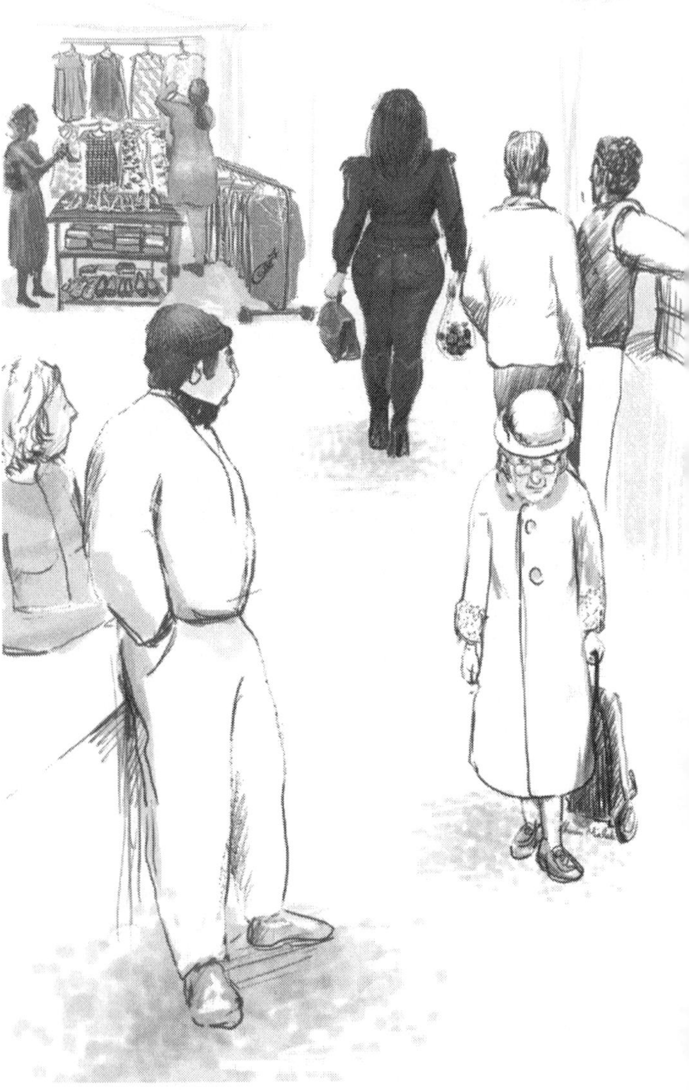

He's referring to the slang that one of our South African customers said once, that in his country they call a nice, pretty girl a mango, and those who imagine themselves incorrectly are called a coconut.

Because of this, whenever Clanzy sees a nice girl passing through, he shouts out "mango…", and the other sellers in the know will turn to have a look.

I don't approve of this secret code, but once you're on the ship, you have to go the way the wind takes you…

Actually, I try to be fair, it's in the nature of the job. All day long you engage with people, maybe you'll make eye contact and that might lead to a sale…

If I was in Iran, I would never have the street trader's life. I don't know, maybe the sellers in the markets of Iran have their own code too…

"Well, she's coming back tomorrow, there's always an excuse to come and see someone.

"Stop it Clanzy, please." I tried to smile.

Clanzy laughs loudly and goes over to tell Peter his version of this story.

***

Saturdays should be for relaxing, having fun or partying, but these days they're all about making money for me.
I mean – my customers buy my sweets and olives for pleasure, fun and parties, while I take their money to pay my bills.
Last Saturday, I made nearly Five hundred pounds, which was just fine.
But the other Saturday, I woke up completely bored of selling olives…! Those kinds of days are worse than days of working for someone else….
After all, if you work for someone else, you can make an excuse to bunk off.
I want to ring up and say I'm sick, I need a day off, and still get paid…I am sick, but I can't make that call.

I wake late again this particular morning, I dress reluctantly and get in the van.

I'm not even in the mood for music. When I get to the market, the other sellers all have customers, and I've only just got my barrow out of the lock-up.

The barrow, or mobile stall that I call a barrow, is a kind of table with wheels and a roof that folds up. It has two metal handles that I pull up to fix it to a column. I usually put a light green striped awning up, and a wooden table nearly three metres wide. Underneath this, just above the wheels, twenty centimetres off the floor, there's another wooden shelf where I can store my other stuff.

White numbers are drawn inside white rectangles on the market floor. I'm number sixty seven, right in the middle. Heaving a wood and metal barrow is quite a strange chore.

If it's rained the previous night, and the floor is muddy, I feel like a sad mule, being watched by everyone else who did this an hour ago. I don't roll up my awning like some of the others, I leave it down overnight…

The first few days, once I finished and took my barrow to the lock up, Clanzy advised me to roll up the awning – it was a fancy one, which looked expensive. He said it would get stolen. But it's heavy and I can't roll it by myself every day.

I risked it! And still it's there every morning, safe

and sound, on top of my barrow. The outside of the awning is dark blue, and the inside is cream…I'd like a car like this, cream leather seats with a dark blue metallic bodywork.

I place a checkered cloth on the table, long enough to reach the street to set off my stall. I put the wooden buckets on one side of the table, along with other containers, then trays of pastries the other side.

* * *

—— My days in London

"Hello, may I ask you something?"
She looks nervous and anxious. A middle-aged woman wearing a long bead necklace, her gray hair forming a triangle shape on her forehead. She speaks English well, but I'm not sure if it's here first language.
"Sure, what?"
"Can I give you my name and phone number, so I can buy some olives and pay you on Tuesday? I've spent all my cash at the farmer's market…"
I smile and nod while she speaks.
"No need to give me your number, what would you like today? Just pay me next time you're passing."
"Four different kinds of Olives in two full containers."
She plays with her phone anxiously, probably texting

someone. I wonder if she'd be looking at her phone if she was paying me right now!? I put her things in a bag.

"Here you are. It's eleven pounds altogether, but pay me when you're next passing," I smile.

"What's your name?" she asks shyly.

I tell her but I doubt she'll remember it.

"I'm Hillary. I'll bring you the money on Tuesday."

"I'm here from Wednesday onwards, so no rush," I say.

If she doesn't pay me back, it's alright, but I'm wondering if buying olives is really so important, she'd get them on credit?! If I sold bread, or vegetables, it would be more understandable…I'm trying to analyze her.

Character analysis is an interesting tool. A woman buys olives on credit! Does she have a really important dinner party? She could use her credit card to get cash, to spare her blushes! Huh, maybe she's thinking why pay extra to use her credit card, when she can get a load of free olives and never be seen again…

Maybe I'm wrong and over-thinking it!

***

On Saturday, I'm waiting for a regular who only ever buys anchovy stuffed olives from me. A middle-aged man who once asked specially for them; I didn't have any that week, but I promised him some the week after. He says his partner likes them. This type of olive is imported from Spain, it's impossible to get them anywhere else, plus selling them is risky. You can't leave olives with fish in in the sun, and they don't keep for long. Once you've opened them, you have to sell them quickly or throw them away, and not that many people like fish in olives.
I like to stand out, so I told him I'll bring the stuffed olives next week, like a pro, and he promised to

come back next week to get them. Here he is with his partner and another boy. His partner is a kind, sincere middle-aged woman, whose son has a disability. It's clear that the boy and the woman have a pre-arranged pact: the man pays for his partner's favorite olives, and the woman takes out her cash to buy sweets for her son.

I don't approve of these arrangements, which are sneaky, even if they're the result of long discussions or arguments. I don't care if that makes me eastern, just go ahead and say it! I really can't bear it and I want to tell them not to do it in front of me.

They should do it in private at least. They can count their money at home, or write it all down in a book to count it at the end of the month. I'm not sure, maybe they're not together just for the money…I don't get it!

It seems like the man is stingy…Even when his partner isn't with him, he says fill the bowls with olives.

My mum's voice: "You don't know the full story, don't judge."

"My dear mum, I'm not judging, I'm just giving my opinion".

***

— My days in London

A tall, pretty woman who asks questions about everything except the price, buys a big bowl of olives and a big bowl of sweets, asking "Where are you really from? Italy or Greece?"
"Neither, I'm Iranian."
"Khoob hastid shoma?" she asks, laughing.
"How do you know Persian?" I ask, astonished.
"I lived in Iran for three years before the Islamic Revolution actually", she answers in English.
"Can I be nosey and ask why?"
"My husband is Iranian, and my son's name is Shahram."
It seems funny, a mother who can't pronounce her son's name properly…
"Now I know you're Iranian, let me ask you one

question – when I was in Iran, I ate a dish that was just like pottage, and when they were cooking it, they put a something a bit like a big block of cheese in, until it melted…"

"I've got no idea what you're talking about."

"Maybe it was a local specialty, I'm not sure…I'll check with my husband and let you know."

I casually remove a long hair from one of the olive bowls, without her noticing.

"Have a nice day."

"You too."

John is an old English man with white hair and a beard, who sells a variety of breads for cafes from his truck. He comes towards my stall with a mellifluous laugh, pointing to the trays of sweets and colourful creams.

"Are these custard?" he says.

"No, they're lemon creams."

"How much for the tray?"

"It's twenty-nine pounds, but I'll do you a deal," I say with a smile.

I know he'll never pay twenty nine pounds for a tray of sweets.

"You're selling sweets the price of Gold!?" he says, laughing.

"You have to pay for quality!" I smile.

The bald Turkish man who works in the front café kitchen comes towards John to greet him.

"How are you?" asks John.

"Not too bad, but I miss my wife, I'm waiting for her, but no news," he answers.

As I take the covers off the sweets, I think back to my first days in this country, and my English teacher telling me that when an English person asks "How are you?", you should answer "Very well, thanks, what about you?" even if you've just been bankrupted, or one of your relations has had a terrible accident! Everyone does it, and they ask you this in every situation, just to be polite…they actually don't really care how you are!?

"Your wife lives with her family?" John asks, as the man explains.

I discover from their chat that the Turkish guy married a girl from his own country, and he's waiting for her visa to come through so she can come here and live with him. I seem to be the third party overhearing very private information!

The Turkish guy asks John how the British Home office checks documents. It's been six months, what is the process? Which paperwork is the most important? Why is it the most important?

John's not in the mood, but smiles and says "you know as much as I do."

His complacency irritates me. "John's never had to apply for UK residency. He never had to get a spousal visa for his wife!" I say loudly, laughing.

"My wife's family didn't want a visa from me…" John laughs.
I have no idea when the Turkish chef left my stall, but I think if someone was asking about applying for residency in Iran, I would have no idea where they would go…
If someone asks me, I would probably say do we even allow foreign people to be residents?!
"Well, John. Do you want the sweets or not?"
"Yes. Give me six pieces of this shiny gold treasure."
"Lemon cream?"
"Yes, that's great."
"Here you are, be my guest…"
"No, tell me how much."
"Five pounds, but three to you."
"Thanks, I hope they're as delicious as the price!"
I laugh.

* * *

"Your nougat was so nice, I'll be back for them again", a smiling blonde woman yells across the street.
I don't remember her coming, or what she bought!
Some people are very noisy, especially when they really like something…I really enjoy hearing women laugh. When women laugh…when my mother laughs…I feel like all is well, all is calm and there is peace in the world…It's hard to explain the sense of tranquility it brings.

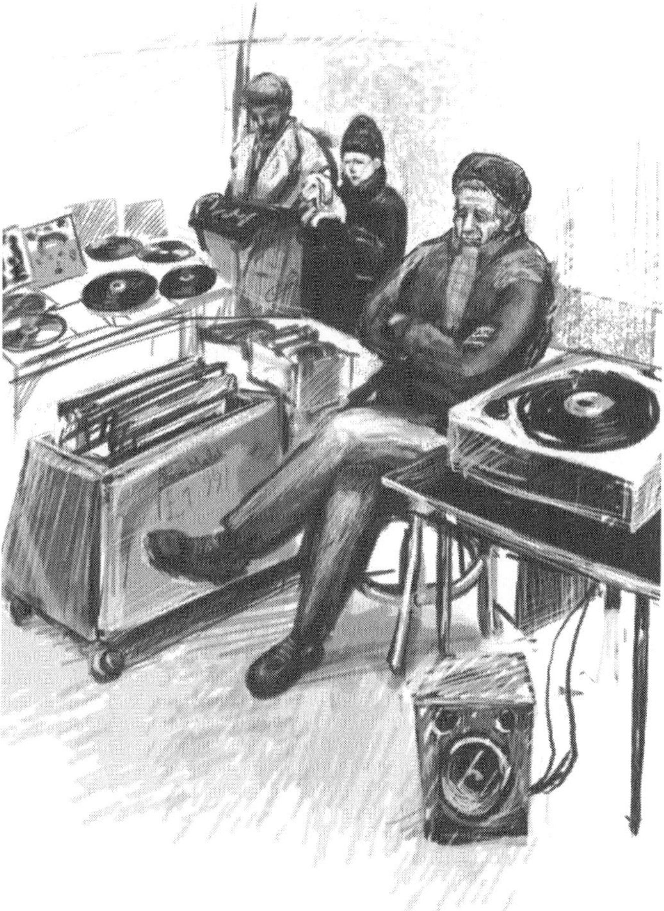

"Duh duh duh duh duh duh duh duh duh, hoo hoo hoo hoo, magic techniques, dari dee dee dee."

I like Jacob. He's a kind old man who conveys a sense of security and peace just with a look…He sells vintage albums and he buys CDs of old original albums that younger people have no interest in, very cheap or even free, and sells them at the market. He's made portable wooden shelves and ranked them by genre. He plays a different kind of music every day, based on his mood, especially Sway. I imagine him as Dean Martin! Maybe he has one of those old vintage cars from the 50's parked in from of his house…I imagine him as one of those people who really knows what love means! Who can hear the sound of the violins long before it starts!
When Marimba rhythms start to play
Dance with me, make me sway
Love should tire you out, bring an unconscious smile and warmth to the voice; it should make you weak, your legs go floppy, and you say:
Like a lazy ocean hugs the shore…
Jacob draws in the customers with his loud voice every now and then…
"It's an original, just one pound and ninety-nine pence!"
How can a songwriter be deeply in love and not bring sexuality to their song and to the love story?!

I believe these people truly understand the meaning of Love!

I imagine Dean Martin and Rosemary Clooney singing this song, both singing for each other from beginning to end:

Other dancers may be on the floor

Dear, but my eyes will see only you

Only you have that magic technique...

Then, Dean sings the same song for Rosemary:

Other dancer may be on the floor

Dear, but my eyes will see only you...

Then, both turn to audience and sing for them, too...

Smoke rises from the Lebanese Falafel seller's grill, the smell of fried onion wafts from the hot dog stand, and the sunlight dances on the corners of the buildings...

Dean Martin croons again:

Only you have that magic technique

And says stay with me...

The smell of fresh fried garlic mixed with the smell of vegetables from the Chinese restaurant...It reminds me of the movie "In the Mood for Love", the yellows and reds, the lights and the sunshine...It reminds me of love.

I sense how lonely Jacob is at the market...

How people like Jacob are so alone at this point in time. I think everyone feels homesick at times in their life, in this world…I leave my stall to ask Jacob whether he has my song. It would be nice if he played it just for us. And then when he changes CD, he'll yell again: "it's original, one pound and ninety-nine pence!"

The happy, blonde woman returns with a beautiful brown dog and the same smile, saying loudly "I'm getting a manicure but I'll be back soon. I'm going to my mother's. I want some of those black olives today." But when she comes back, she points to the coconut sweeties. "Look, there are those delicious nougat sweets."

I don't tell her they're actually coconut.

"I'm a cook myself, I should be able to make these but I can't. Did I tell you, I cook for a family in Notting Hill Gate? The woman is Danish and the man is Lebanese. They're very rich and pay very well. I work Monday to Friday, and also prep their food for the weekend, I have to label everything for them" she laughs loudly and carries on… "I like my job."

One of the problems of having regulars is that you can't just weigh their orders, tell them the price and take your money. You have to chat with them, and the interactions can be irritating for me...

She leans in as if to tell me a secret...

"When you work for...Sorry, where are you from?"

She wants to make sure I'm not Danish or Lebanese.

"Iran."

"Okay, right. I was going to say that working for Middle Eastern people is a pain despite the money."

She makes a statement about Middle Eastern people, but I don't get it. She's generalizing about Middle Eastern people and their whole character!

"What do you mean by that?"

"Um, it means they expect a lot for their money. They pay well, but they expect you to work hard. For instance, you don't have fixed hours, if you think you'll finish at five, you'll probably be there till eight."

"Aha! I get it...I know."

I change the subject, not sure why...

"What a cute dog you have!"

"Oh, this is their dog, I know, she's really cute. They're away travelling. Oh, she's such a good girl!"

"Yes, she is cute."

***

I'm thinking about how much my life has changed when a car rushes by, pumping out loud music. Without looking at the car or the driver, I guess there goes Pretty-eyes.

He's a black guy, initially I thought he was Indian, but he doesn't hold himself like someone from India. He runs a stall selling bedspreads, blankets and sheets.

I noticed his 'pretty eyes' when he first took off his sunglasses, they were small and sunken. It's too hard to speak to him face to face without glasses.

He's had this Mini for quite a while…it used to be a nice brown colour, but after a couple of weeks he pimped it up to have a ridiculous horn that sounds like a barking dog, or a rooster, and long plastic eyelashes above the front lights.

He's written "Kiss me once more baby" on the hood, and on the rear windscreen he's written his email address, in a terrible font, 'Ricky brown sugar, @....' That was how I found out he's called Ricky! Ricky has a friend called Jeffrey, and they are a terrible match.

Jeffrey seems a little deranged, not really all there; but I say hi, even though there's no sign of pretty-eyes! It's not our first encounter. One time, in the early days, I was selling packs of cashews in four flavours: chili, honey, cinnamon and smoky, and he came to buy from me. I said they were two pounds each, but just one to you; he says "Great, I'll have five, two with honey and one of each of the others."

I was kicking myself as I got out my change. "Idiot! why did you give him a discount? You've sold them the same price you bought them!" But anyway, since then I've always said hello or good morning when I see Jeffrey, but never anything to Ricky.

It goes back to my first day on the market, when I was looking for my allocated pitch number. I didn't know that the numbers weren't in order, and I was looking for the 67th one. I thought that Ricky's bedspread stall was mine.

I went to tell them it should be for me. It was Jeffrey who said "Rubbish! we've been here for three years. Let me see your license." When I showed him, he said this is the 64th, you're 67th just the other side of the street, further up. I apologised and went to find it.

The next time I was pulling my stand past the bedspread stall, I said good morning; but pretty-eyes was taking the mickey, this is my spot, this is my spot, goofing about like an idiot, and it upset me; that's no way to welcome a new seller, especially a novice like me! I really didn't appreciate the joke.

I went for him – "You think you're a big guy, huh?! Are you taller, tougher, what? why are you taking the piss?!"

Thinking back, I'm not sure I said this in English, but I'm sure my feelings were clear!

Since then, we don't acknowledge each other! The

other thing is that he has three cars, in a country where buying a car is much easier than maintaining it.

His mini is mainly for parking in the market for girls to take selfies with, booming out music. My English customers always laugh: enjoy the free Disco!

I'm not sure whether it's an Eastern view or not, but what's with putting a big speaker in a small car, no thought for your own ears or others?! On Sunday, pretty-eyes comes in an SUV Porsche, which he parks for everyone to see while he gets his milky tea from the café; then he'll get back in and park it somewhere else, while Jeffrey is stuck alone on the stall with all his stuff. He has a Toyota rav4 to bring his new bedspreads and sheets in. He had a BMW for nearly two weeks; whenever the Turkish guy from the café saw it, he'd say "That car's no good", and Pretty-eyes would yell across the street "What? You jealous? You are, you're jealous!" I've got no idea how he can run three cars, all needing insurance and petrol, just from selling bedspreads and sheets!

He's going to end up bankrupt…

My mind is wandering again. Ah, my life changed right after the internet came to Iran, which led to my visit to London to see Feri years later.

In fact, all of this happened because I learned how to connect the phone to a modem and dial up; that dial up noise followed by a promising silence meant I was con-

_____ My days in London

nected to a totally new world, very far from anything I'd seen or heard before. Feri was working in a chain store. They were younger than me, but their life was more exciting than mine as I was out of work. I read books and watched movies, while they went to the amusement park and won dolls. I'd stay up all night and go to bed just as they woke up for work. They'd have a coffee and blueberry muffin for breakfast, all I knew was that a blueberry was a small blue fruit, nothing more. I had my coffee with dark chocolate, and wished I knew what this blue fruit tasted like; they promised me that if I got on a plane and came to visit, they'd take me to the closest café to get a big cup of coffee and a blueberry muffin. Six months later, there I was in a plane; six hours after that, I was having a big cup of coffee and a blueberry muffin at Heathrow Airport, terminal 4.

I can't think why I didn't have the coffee and blueberry muffin, and get a plane straight back, back to my life of late sleeping, books and movies?!
But they'd made some other promises.
"Have you got a spare cigarette?"
I think they promised me a better life.
"What? Ah....no, I don't."
Michael is a thin alcoholic who asks me at least three times a day if I have a spare cigarette. I want to tell him I've got nothing spare except my brain which I'm not really using here in the market! But I need all my other stuff! Especially this damn cigarette!
Michael gets five pounds per day from Peter as a wage, because he pulls Peter's plant racks from the lock-up to the market every morning, for half an hour. It turns into a bottle of one-pound beer and a packet of ten cigarettes immediately. Still, he'll continually ask for a cigarette; I give him one when I feel like it, and sometimes I surprise him with one when he doesn't ask. My reasoning is that I can't give up both my cigarettes and my free will!

***

I wish it could last forever, with the one who was your better love...

I put my hand in my trousers' pocket, open the cigarette packet, take one and put it to my lips, take my lighter from my other pocket. I can really feel my body craving Nicotine today. Every cigarette I smoke seems like the first one...

"From the first day I knew that you'd leave..." the singer sings.

I had a smile on my lips when I got up this morning. It's weird! I've been waking up with remorse lately. I put on the clothes I wore yesterday, but I feel handsome. I made coffee in a hurry, and while I was sipping it, I change the source of the music from the speakers to my headphones, and imagine it playing live in the room.

"Your happiness is my wish…if the one who is with you loves you more, if you are convenient with that person, and if supports you…"

I hastily put on my shoes and get out. I need fresh air. The wind feels nice.

I wish it could last forever, with the one who was your better love…

***

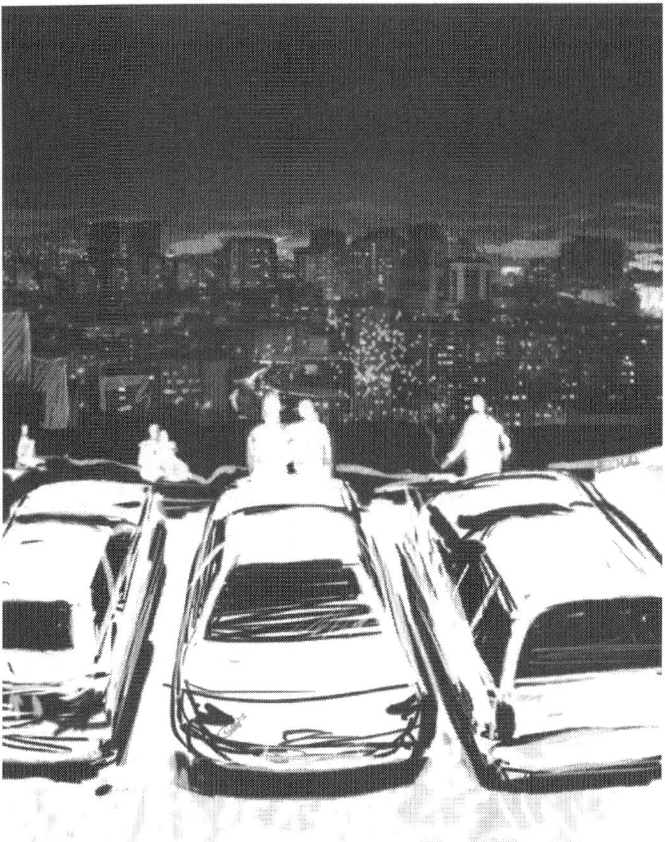

I decide I'll go to the top of the hill at Alexandra Palace to listen to this song again after work. I wonder how different the view of the city will look, to the first time I found it. I go by car and park, have a coffee and listen to the music while gazing at the city lights.

I have a sense of missing something...

I used to go to the mountains every night in those days. I'd pass the thin strip of mountains in the early evening, get to the top and park in front of the Tehran landscape. I poured coffee from the flask I'd brought, smoked and thought and thought....and thought.

Now in another part of the world, I found another hill to see the city from, but I don't even know what

I'm looking for this time, and it's ridiculous to be thinking about another view, place and country.

Maybe if this carries on, I'd end up finding more hills in cities of the world and indulge in sitting and viewing them!

I think it's all over for a person, when they've reached rock bottom like me.

"Sometimes you should die to make a new life…" the singer sings!

I think only when I die will there be no need for a hill. I'll be able to see the world from up on high, I'll look at all the lights of the cities all over the world from there.

Surely we all go upwards into the sky, right?!…

***

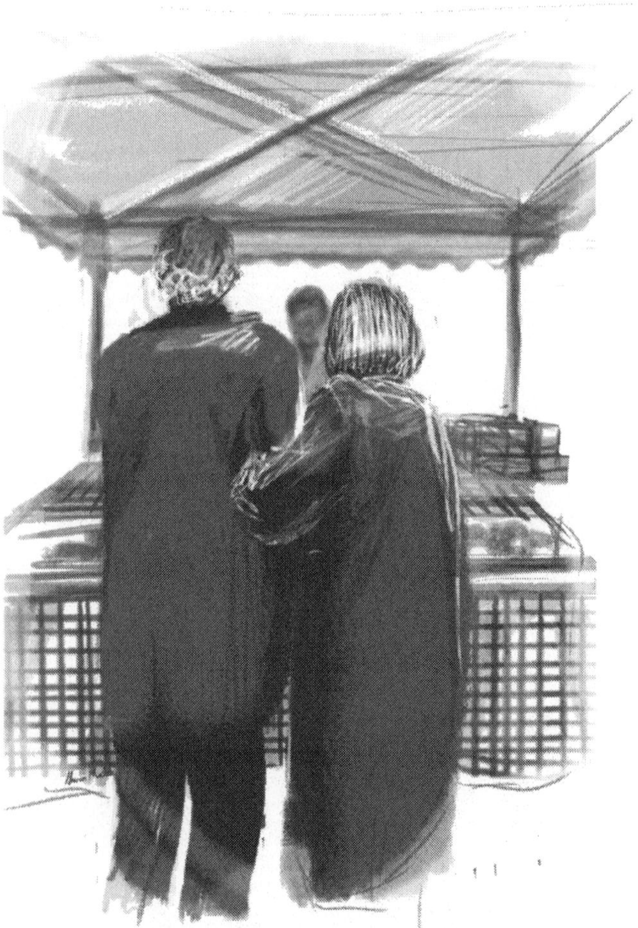

The old woman and man often come to my stall hand in hand…

"Buon Giorno."

What I mean is, the old woman holds her hand around the old man's arm. The first time they bought something from me, the man was pulling the woman towards the stall as if he knew it would make her happy! It was obvious that he was so elderly he could hardly speak. He just points to the sweets, indicating he wants two of each. It occurs to me that young people usually only buy one of each.

I give them two of each flavour, and without telling them, I give them a big discount, but even so I'm sure it's a lot of money for them. The old woman, who must have been very pretty when she was young, thinks it's pricey!

But the old man pays twenty pounds straight away, and the old woman, who is possibly has very bad eyesight, takes the sweets.

When they go, I remember the movie "Love" by Michael Haneke. I confess that I've never seen such a relationship between elderly Iranian couples. But that could be because I never had a market stall in Iran!

I'm sure this film could be broadcast on Iranian TV uncensored; it doesn't need translating, because the love should be felt, and it's palpable.

This time the old man says "two of each, two of each…"

"I think it's too much!" the old woman says.

"I agree with your wife. I'm here every day, and it's better to buy a few and have them fresh!" I add.

I know I'll never be a good salesman when I'm worried about other people's pockets; some may not have any problems with money after all. But the old woman's delight at the final cost made me happy.

***

One of the best experiences of my life was the time I spent 36 hours in a cargo ship, from Tilbury Docks in the UK to the port of Gutenberg. I wanted to go to Stockholm as part of the sales team of an Iranian company, to sell baklava at a two-week festival.

It was a wonderland surrounded by sea, the only other passengers were truck drivers, and we settled in a small, quiet corner of the ship, set aside just for us. I will never forget the taste of mango tea, mixed with the smell of the sea, and the story of the book 'Breaking Away' by Anna Gavalda that I was reading lying down on the deck.

It was then I realized that nature is stronger than man; I mean, the earth is round and gravity pulls the water to the earth, so now I'm on a ship, it's as if I'm floating on the earth. It made me think of the fragility of a spider's web!

At the Swedish market, I see I've forgotten my mobile and my watch, so I lose track of time and before

I know it the market is starting up.

When I open the front covers, I see I didn't need my watch anyway, because the church clock is right in front of me, how dim that was that it took me two weeks to notice! It's a long way off, but the steeple is tall enough that I could see every second pass…

I think when they built this Church, they must have known that one day I'd be here selling baklava! The Swedish were conspiring to mess with my head…

The sun had set, and a cold wind was blowing from my right.

I wore a jumper over clothes I'd already worn. Someone said our work is just like farming, fighting with nature, against the wind, rain and snow to get money!

Come and try…Don't be shy…This sweet Baklava….

I repeat myself over and over, laughing. I have to pretend to be happy, one of the miseries of my job! The more fun you bring, the more you will sell…

Yes…Yes! This is Lebanese baklava…it's so delicious, trust me…. yes, this is Kataifi roll with pistachio and honey.

On occasion, I stare into space. I didn't know what was going on around me until someone made me snap out of it.

"Are you asleep? Give out some samples! It seems like you're not with it today!"

It seemed just like any other day, so why's the guy from the company here, checking my work, asking "Are you okay?"

Maybe I'm no good at this.

"There's no one to give samples to", I answer.

"Yell louder, and they'll come", he says.

After several goes of yelling and giving out samples, I had a word with myself, stay on the ball, you can't lose this one.

You want to sleep in the street again?! I need to stop grumbling and remember that, because I didn't want the life I had before. There were many people who wanted to listen, but no one could help me….

I sit on a chair to think. Sometimes the sound of my sobbing scares me, and in those moments the concerned and sympathetic look of kind people who would listen to my words makes me calm down and live in the moment! I know I'm too strong to be crushed up…

"Give out some samples!" the manager said.

* * *

I missed a day of work last week, even though it started off a day like any other. I mean I got up and got in the van, but I got stuck in traffic for an hour and a half, and every route towards Archway was closed. Even if the traffic got lighter, it was now too late and pointless! So I turned round and went back home. After that, I heard on the news that someone had thrown oneself off the bridge and taken his own life, which caused the traffic!
I say to Peter "That person was the reason I was late and lost money! If someone wants to end it all, why can't they do it in their own home instead of making it a pain for everyone else?"
But Peter has a convincing answer. He says that that last night he was so tired he almost fell on the train

tracks!

"Maybe it wasn't a suicide, he could have been so tired he slipped, or had an accident, but everyone think it is a suicide!"

"Whatever, it's an accident that cost me two hundred pounds", I say to Peter.

"Why don't you look on the bright side? It made you take a day off and get some rest."

* * *

"I want three pounds of these garlic with cheese in, and the same of this garlic, too", the woman says. I put the cheese olives in a bowl with a capacity of 750 cc, and I carefully fill just half the dish to add the garlic, when she says "less, less than that…"

I try and control myself. I look at her and say "you want three pounds, right?!"

She looks very plain, as if she doesn't even comb her hair.

"If that's less than three pounds, that's no problem, that's enough", she said.

There can't be more than eleven olives here!

I turn my head. It's the man with gray hair who I had a nice chat with. He hides behind the woman. He wears that cream coat that doesn't reach his knees. I warmly say hello, but he answers coldly. The whole connection I had with him is interrupted by

_____ My days in London

the woman's body. As if the woman came to teach him how resist the skills of a salesman and spend less money…or maybe he has a problem with me!
Three weeks ago when he came, I was putting sweets on the table. "Are you ready right now?" he asks.
"It's never too early to take your money", I say.
"I bought those olives with cheese in, they were so tasty", he laughs and says.
While I'm serving, he asks "Where are you from?"
We start to talk about different people and cultures. While I put the garlic in a smaller dish, I explain that I saw a film called "The Stanford Prison Experiment" last night. At the time, I lose get carried away explaining the film to the man with the gray hair, and he listens intently.
Briefly, the story of the film is that newspaper ads were published, requesting volunteers for a two-week psychology experiment; 14,000 dollars would be paid. So 1000 dollars a day, no experience needed, and it was completely safe. The researchers chose 26 volunteers, and took them to a place very much like a jail. Some of them were given prisoners' uniforms, and the others warders' uniform. They set distinct rules for each group, and watched as their behavior changed terribly over only a few hours.
I say that the film showed the noticeable and surprising psychological effects of power.
As we talk about power, the characteristics of peo-

ple who like power, and its effects on their soul, the man asks "How much are my olives?"

"Fifteen pounds". I put them on the scale.

"I don't think I should buy a big bowl of each", he said, looking at the change in his hand.

"How much do you want to spend? I'll give you that amount", I say.

"Nine pounds." He counts out the pound coins.

"Sure."

I open his dish, take a bit from each one to put back, and while I'm handing him the dish and taking the coins, we say goodbye.

"I've enjoyed chatting to you."

"Me too".

"Hope you do well today!"

"Thanks", I laugh.

After he leaves, I think about our chat for a long time…I go to get a big cappuccino from the café with the beautifully displayed baguettes. While I stand by the stall, puffing on a cigarette and sipping my cappuccino, I wondered "is it possible to show the film in Iran, with a few cuts and dubbing…"

A drunk man distracts me from my thoughts about the man with the cream Jacket.

"Where are you from?"

"I'm from Unvare Donya!"

I like saying this to nosey people.

"Where is Unvare Donya?"

"In a rich country in the Middle East".
"So you're rich then?"
"No, I live in London and sell olives!" Missing my point, he wiggles past my booth and I pull my chair closer to sit down.

I remember the time that I told a man I'm Iranian, he laughed; and when I asked "What about you? Where are you from", he said "Promise not to kill me? I'm Israeli."

It was like being on a tiny Italian Island, and hearing a church bell in the silence. I thought that even if the sky is blue everywhere, it doesn't matter because I don't live in the sky!

***

I don't know if categorizing things is due to having a knack for math or physics. I want to know if I'm interested in math or physics because I like to categorize my thoughts into groups. I even choose a lead category to start with, to make my thinking extra clear…I'm probably in the fourth generation of Iranians in such a category.

It's different to using a pen and paper. That's what I like about it, because it exercises a part of my mind, the categorizing par that I used to use in the past. My mind is categorizing this way when I look at Minoo. She's a friend of Feri. On a day at the market that was so cold, my glass of tea sticks to my lips, and I'm thinking that this work is keeping me from my already hard studies because of being in a different language.

already hard because they're in a different language. I see Minoo pass with a big bag on wheels.

Minoo lives close to the Market Street. Every time she passes my stall, we say hello and chat. Today she stands in the middle of the street, two metres away from my stall, stopping to say hello.

"It's so cold. How can you stand there all day long?"

"Got to make a living", I laugh.

Chilled to the bone, I say "I've got plenty of clothes on…you get used to it, if you do it every day."

"Do people really buy your stuff in this cold weather? In the market? Surely they'd prefer a shopping centre, I don't know, somewhere more enclosed!"

I showed her my notes that I keep by the scales.

"I'm writing an essay for my Uni course, and if anyone wants anything, I'm right here".

"What are you studying? How's University?" she asks while standing two metres closer then

As Minoo asks, I sob and my eyes suddenly fill with tears.

I take a sip of tea to suppress my sob…it was so hard to hold it in.

My reading glasses are next to my notes, so I put them on to make my eyes look normal…

"With this job it's impossible. I think I have to choose one or the other."

Minoo talks about perseverance, and her time of

being a student along with the entire second generation. I pretend to listen, but I'm answering her in my head. For example, when she says that taking a Major will make you learn English, and living the student life means you're not forced to work hard…I answer in my head that it was free to study in England in your time, the Government paid your tuition and rent, so you only had to study and get a part time job for some extra cash…

In my head I tell Minoo that even in my university notebook, during class, I make lists of how I need to buy more popular olives, or how can I sell them! "To be honest, it's pointless educating me, this is the second time I've left Uni", I laugh and say.

When I'm honest with myself, I admit that I'm working every day except Monday, and I study part time three days a week! After work, I only have time to wash my face, put on some perfume and go, but the smell of Olives is overwhelming…

If she tells me I should work less, I'll say that I wouldn't be able to pay my rent, the commuting costs, and some of my bills! Also, I'm studying film and media. Even after four years of training, I won't have access to the industry. I study for the love of it, and I do love to sit in a class with student like me, three days a week, talking about a TV show that was broadcast live like a theatre show!

If only it was just this, but no. You have to take exams, and write a 3000 word essay every week. They never allow you to just enjoy it.

I was wondering whether to give up studying or not?! So I wouldn't be in debt to the Government in vain. Minoo's answer is clear. The English side of her character, the side that has lived here in London for 21 years says only you can decide, it's your life! And her Iranian side, from the second generation says why you are like this (?) You, a new young arrival from Iran, you want everything handed to you on a plate! You're indifferent to your own life!

This time I want to say: see, I'm not indifferent, because I'm asking your advice!

Instead, I laugh and say "we are fourth generation!" As I look at the surprise in Minoo's face, I continue "We're the generation who…"

The sob that I swallowed came back up again. I took another sip of tea, and with a smile in my voice I say "We are the generation that were told when we were studying – You're in a rich country, we have minerals, farmland, culture, we have four seasons, and so we thought we had everything and there was no need to do anything, we were just there to enjoy the fruits of the previous generations labour".

"To be honest, dear Minoo, we became a lazy and passive generation with expectations that are too high!" I laugh loudly.

Minoo still looks amazed. She tries to laugh but raises her eyebrows and asks: "Which generation are we then?"

Without reflecting I say "second".

"You are the generation with perseverance, who want to fix things that aren't okay, and when you look back on your lives you see that you worked the whole time. There are so many successful people in your generation, but no one realizes that they are highly qualified and happy in their lives…"

***

"Oh yeah! Are these those famous bright green Sicilian olives?" asks a pregnant woman, who turns out to be American...
"Do you want to try one?"
"How can I resist them!" she laughs. "Yes. That's it.... Italian night tonight! I'll make Lasagne which will be amazing with these olives". She tries one.
"Enjoy, have a perfect evening!"
I've never been to Sicily, but when customers ask why these olives are so green, I tell them that they grow on the tree like this, people love them! They're fresh with no added oil, just soaked in water and salt. I said they grow on the tree, but really they grow on little twigs sprouting from some olives like a greengage with a little seed.

The first time I tried these Sicilian olives was at a music festival in Festival. The Olive booth was next to mine, where I was selling baklava. The managers of the olive company saw I was doing good business in baklava, so wherever I stood was a good spot!

I was given nearly 20 types of Lebanese baklava to sell, all with different aromas and flavours. Cinnamon, cardamom and saffron baklava, in different shapes and sizes, with pistachio, cashew, almond and walnuts in them…

When I travel to some countries, the Turkish, Syrian, Greek, Arabic and even Iranian customers tell me that the baklava of their own countries are better than these, but they buy them anyway because they miss the familiar taste of home…

There were a group of us at the company who travelled mostly at weekends, over three or four days, and each of us had a different item to sell. Dried fruit and nuts in one booth, Italian biscuits, nougat, chocolate, and at the end, the olive booth. The person in charge, who had to check on everyone else's work, was normally put in charge of Olives for some reason. When I started to buy and sell olives myself, I saw that the profits on Olives are much better than the other things, so you put your best salesman on olives if you want to make a profit.

* * *

"What's this, Mozarella?"
"No, it's garlic mixed with mashed paprika!"
"Wow…"
"What about this?"
"It's an Italian sweet with vanilla cream in, a bit like a croissant".
"How much is this?"
"The price is on it – It's four pounds fifty for 250 grams.
"You mean I can't buy just one?"
"Sure, but I have to weight it. For example, each one of these will be fifty pence".
The customer leaves then.
I shout "thank you!" after him as he goes down the path, meaning, you should be thanking me for my time, even if you're not going to buy anything!

* * *

A rotund woman who looks Eastern European comes towards my booth with a smile.
"Can I have two of these?"
I wrap the sweets and put them in her hand and take the money. She's still standing and giving me a smile…
"You look happy. Anything happened? Something special?" I ask.
She hardly speaks English and muddles up words all the time.

"Not, actually. I was looking at my face in front of mirror today, I told to myself that I'm so pretty".
She laughs and so do I. I look at a man who's approaching, he's heard the woman's last words and he's smiling.
"You really are pretty, and I wish you happiness…"
I'm sure I've never said these words to myself in front of a mirror in my entire life.
The woman leaves the booth and the man takes her place…
"Could I have two of the baklava, please?"

As I put them in a dish, I ask: "Have you ever looked in the mirror and told yourself how handsome you are?"
"Never", he laughs.
"Me neither. I thought maybe it's weird I've never done it before…" I laugh. We both laugh.
"But you are handsome!" I give him the baklava.
"Thanks, you too!" he laughs.

***

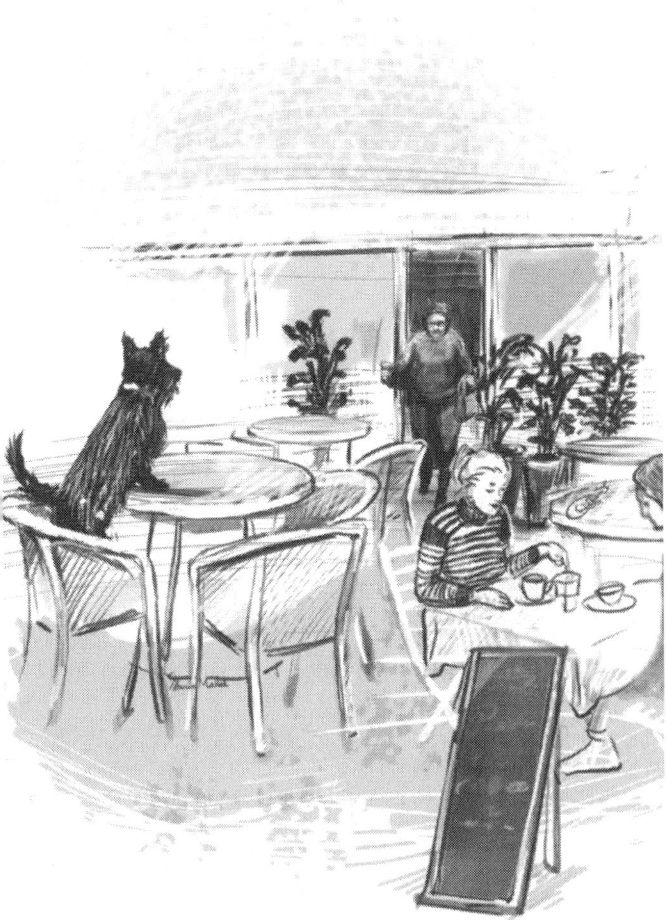

Rocky is sitting on a café chair and barking.
Every time the old woman goes to the café to order, Rocky barks nonstop until she comes back to him…
Two girls pass my booth and see Rocky, sitting there very politely with his front paws on the table, and they laugh.
"He's waiting for his tea and the newspaper he ordered!"
"Yes, I think he's barking because they're not ready yet!"
Leo yells from the other side of the market: "Rocky…Rocky be quiet!"
Rocky stops barking for a moment…the old woman comes out of the café with a newspaper and a cup of tea.
"Who's a good girl?"
The old woman must be nearly seventy. Most of her hair has fallen out, and what's left is pure white.
She says Rocky is her world! Even when she goes to work, she takes Rocky with her. I don't know what she did when she was young, but after retiring, she decided to start working again, now she's a cleaner for the offices next to the market, and she works a few days a week.
She sits outside the café even in winter, because the owner doesn't allow any animals inside, even a little pet like Rocky…

***

I hear Clanzy yell out "Thanks!"

I can tell someone came and asked a load of questions, all the prices, and then walked off.

A tall, well-dressed English woman, who looks very familiar, comes towards my booth.

"Oh, hello. I love that baklava of yours! Could you put six of them in this small dish for me?"

"How about I put them in this large one? I can't fit more than four baklava in this dish!"

"Oh, ok. Give me four then, I'll come back midweek. You know what, the first thing I do in bed in the morning is eat these baklava!"

"Really? You keep them near your bed?!" I laugh.

"No! When I wake up in the morning, my husband goes down to the kitchen, and he comes back up with a tea or coffee and a couple of these big, delicious baklava!" she laughs.

"Enjoy! Have a lovely day!"

"Thanks darling, it's so wonderful you're here, don't go anywhere else, please!"

I laugh.

* * *

Michael comes up to me to show me the shock-horror part of the Metro, something about a murder last night…I know what he really wants is a cigarette. I give him a cigarette.

"I don't want a cigarette. I want to show you the

news! Ok, thanks, I'll have it, but I'll smoke it later".
I see him light his cigarette as he's leaving.
I think if you didn't want a cigarette, you wouldn't have come over here!"
Why would you show a shocking story in the Metro to an impatient Iranian person!"
An old woman slowly comes towards my booth and takes off her glasses to see the sweets properly.
"Could I have two of those chocolate cannoli?"
"Yes, sure".
"Sorry, I forgot my manners! Could I have those please?"
"Here you are. I hope you like them", I smile.
"Thanks sweetie!"
"You're welcome. Have a nice day. Take care".

* * *

I'll go back to Iran…
The words came into my head a while ago, I made my plans. I felt happy, but when I'm thinking practically, I think what on earth will I do there? I can't go there and sell olives in the street, and I haven't got enough money to get a shop! I decide I'll spend time saving money, so I can buy a shop in Iran and live there. Importing Greek olives is ridiculous, when we can use green olives from Roodbar, with walnut and pomegranate in them?!

Times like this remind me of Vahid. I saw him in the pizza shop. He lived without a visa or any other documents, not even an Iranian passport, and he worked illegally. He slept in the shop at night.

"What kind of life has he got? He should go back to Iran, at least he'll be close to family there!"

"How can I go back to Iran? How would I explain what I've been doing all this time? Are you a doctor or an engineer?"

"Just explain the situation you were in here!"

He said "Emigration is good for three groups. First, those who come here with family as children, and study here. Then those who come here with financial support from Iran, in which case they can make a good life for their children, and their lives are devoted to making things perfect for them, and finally those with nothing to lose, who have no dependents back home to miss you…

I don't think I'm in any of the groups that Vahid described. As a result, I don't count as a successful emigrant, if success equals quality of life!

I think about the fact that when he invited his mother over, he borrowed a wealthy friend's house and car to reassure his Iranian mother that her son had a good life in a foreign country; but I see now that Vahid wants to go back to Iran to his family…

***

I think everyone reaches a point in life where they accept everything is well as is. what they have is enough, they are enough, too. They can't be more than this, it can't be! This is the human stage of accepting fate, the stage of death, death of desire, and I'm comfortable with people who reach this stage because I understand them...I believe that it's in this phase that people gain insight into their own character because there is no rise and fall.
Everything exists on the very spot you're standing, and it doesn't have to mean inertia or emptiness, even if you don't know what to do with your life, yourself and especially your hands...
This acceptance of fate will help you get up in the

morning, and without any stressful ambitions or fear of failure, you can consider planting a tree or small shrub, because you understand you need to replace the oxygen you breathe; or the day after that you can consider buying coffee beans of a higher quality, grind them yourself to make chocolate cake, invite some neighbours round in the evening to fill the air with the smell of coffee and cake, and sit near the tree you planted yesterday to talk about the vain ambition you no longer have…Maybe after that, you get out the barbecue, and instead of cooking meat, you see that it will be better to make mushrooms, tomatoes, asparagus and corn.

* * *

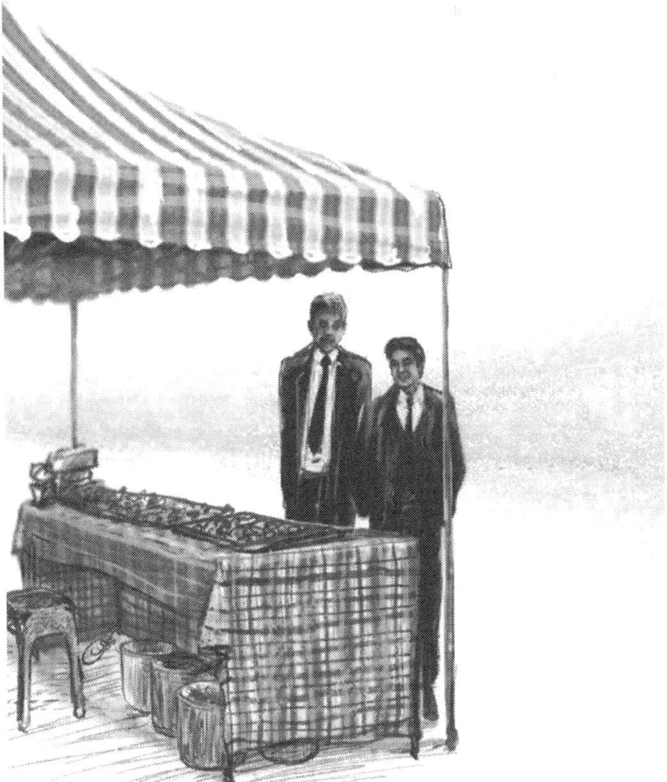

A tall man in a black suit and purple tie, with a million dollar smile, and white, neat, even teeth chats with another man who could be his colleague. He's shorter than him, but his suit looks more expensive; they're here to buy some Italian sweets, and he explains to his colleague that in London there are a few places that sell Cannoli, but these are the most delicious. I laugh.
To me, everyone who works in an office or a bank, and wears the formal uniform of suits and skirt suits looks the same.
My subversive thoughts stay in the background trying not to speak out!
"How many of us are there?"
The man counts his colleagues and says we're eleven.

"Could we buy all eleven of the chocolate cream flavour, please?"

"Sure, why not?!"

I begin counting out the sweets to put in the packet...

"If you had an espresso to go with them that would be perfect! Why don't you get a coffee machine here?"

In a street market, in the wind and rain?! No way! It's impossible to sell hot drinks, It's risky, dangerous even!

But I answer "Brilliant idea! You're absolutely right."

I tell myself "I'm saving up to open a coffee shop, then I can serve these sweets with coffee, while I sit in the corner doing my own writing".

This always makes me laugh.

"Have a nice day".

"Thanks, same to you."

I wonder how long I can stick it out at the market. One day I'll be old...

* * *

I don't know if having a sense of humour is instinctive, or if I should cultivate it? But if I cultivate it, it would be hard work because so many parts are involved – brain, face, mouth and body language. David is one of those people who is instinctively cute, and he puts it into action several times a day!

I remember the sound of his laugh from the first few times I came to the market.

Ha…ha…ha…ha… Ha…ha…ha…ha…

David, the man with the sweet laugh, opens and shuts his stall before everyone else!

He and his wife Pamela have a small booth down there selling fruit, but they display them in an unusual way.

He arranges all the colours in harmony, grouped in glass dishes, and above them he's written "Two for a pound", on a black board with white chalk. Each dish weighs a pound and a half, and he sells out before anyone else.

David makes it clear so people can buy easily, not like my stall where customers are always asking "how many of these in 250 grammes?"

On a red plastic banner above his booth he's written "Dave and Pam, Daily Fresh fruit"

Pam comes to the booth at 9 o'clock in the morning, always done up in make-up and smart clothes, as if she'd been a bank manager in her youth! But I know that David has worked at the market for forty years, so the likelihood of her having a background in management can't be true, so I've stopped thinking about it!

The first time I went to buy fruit from him, he gave me a discount.

"David, don't give me a discount, please. I will always buy fruit from you anyway", I said.

I always wonder why we should give out discounts! And why does a vendor have to stand up all day long?!

It seems like it's the first time someone had refused a discount!

"Where are you from?" he says.

"I'm Iranian", I say.

"Oh, I went there once!"

"Really?"

"Yeah, I went all the way there and it was closed!"

I look at him and we both laugh.

This guy can make anything into a joke.

I saw that Pam wasn't at the stall, and David was putting boxes onto a trolley, to get them to the storeroom for packing...

"Have you really never tried any other job, David? With your sense of humour? You could be a standup comedian or even a showman!" I ask.

"Yes, I tried it once but everyone laughed at me...I was so upset I never tried it again".

He screws up his face and pouts like a kid about to cry, but his eyes are sparkling with mischief.

"See...See...You're amazing!" I laugh and say.

He laughs too and says "You show me a miserable bastard who can display fruit as well as I do...This market needs me!" he blinks.

"I know, I know!" I laugh.

A middle-aged woman comes towards me. I watch her approaching and when she's near enough, I say with a smile "I like your style!"
Her white, wavy hair curls on her forehead, and at the back her fair hair curls onto her shoulders...
Behind her cat-eye glasses, her eyes are enhanced with black eyeliner, perfectly drawn in Kohl pencil, and her eyelashes are curled just like her hair. Her open and cute smile completes her graceful look.
"Oh, thank you!" she answers.
I look at her brown shirt with tiny pleats on the sleeves...
Everything about this woman is simple, graceful and subtle.
"I'd love some olives".

"Would you like to taste some to see which you like best?"

"No, surprise me! I want four pounds worth".

I'll put some olives filled with pomegranate, some green Sicilian Olives, some Kalamata, some chili and a couple of red peppers stuffed with ricotta and blue cheese all in one dish.

"I hope you like them".

"No doubt I will!"

As she's leaving, I notice she's wearing a long, well-made cream skirt over black ankle boots, and a heavy looking Paul smith bag on her left shoulder…

"Here you go, here's your tea".

"Thanks".

Clanzy gives me a cup of tea and goes.

I glance at my watch, it's nearly three in the afternoon. I take the tea bag out and put it in the bin under my table.

I put a piece of one of the broken Cannolis onto a tray to eat with my tea.

"Wow…what a beautiful stall! If my son were here, he'd eat the lot!"

A medium height woman with black wavy hair, high forehead, large eyes and a sweet accent says:

"How much are these?"

"They're eighty pence each!"

"That's too expensive!"

I take one of the broken Cannolis to give her.

"Taste this."

"Are you sure?! I don't know if I can afford anything?!"

"I don't care…no obligation…I eat them, too. The broken ones are samples. Bon apetit! Where are you from? I really like your accent!" I laugh.

"Colombia".

"There's a famous Colombian actress that I love. Her name…her name is Sophia something…"

"Vergara!"

"Yes…yes…yes…Ah, she's amazing!"

She's thrilled! She eats another piece of Cannoli, and so do I. I eat mine with a sip of tea.

She tells me that Sophia's first appearance was in a TV ad for soda, when she was just fifteen, and everyone loved her from then on.

I don't know why but I don't want her to leave! I like the way she says certain words. She puts the last bit of Cannoli in her mouth to get her phone out of her bag, to show me a photo of her son, and says "I got divorced eight years ago. My husband was irresponsible, but our boy is my whole life…I'd like to buy one of these for him. You said eighty pence, right?"

I put two in a packet and say "be my guest".

"You remind me so much of my nephew! Where are you from?"

"I'm Iranian!"

She shows me photos of her nephew…I look at her.

___ My days in London

"How did you end up here? Are you homesick?"
"Yes…Can you believe I haven't been back for twelve years?!"
"Why not?"
"It's so expensive! Two thousand pounds for its ticket!"
"Well, if you book in advance, it's cheaper."
She changes the subject and shows more photos of her family, then goes on Facebook to show me more photos. "My son is at school…"
I'd like to talk to her more…her accent is intriguing, as if she's about to say something funny!
"Well, I should go, and you should get back to your work". She takes her bag.
I laugh.

* * *

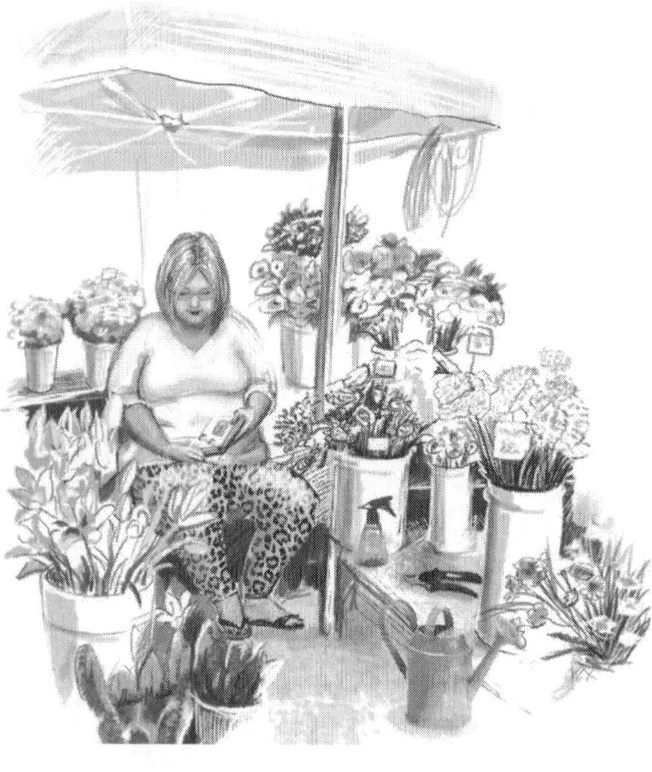

Dana, the florist with a stall on the left of me, is a curvy white woman, with newly highlighted hair. She asks me "what are you smoking?"
It's impossible to imagine her slim however hard, I try. She wears summer flip flops with a white dress and baggy leopard print trousers, and holds an album of different flower arrangements to show her customers what she can do. Whenever she's hungry she goes straight to the jacket potato stand to eat stuffed wedges, or McDonald's; and for desert, she comes to my stand to get a baklava as big as her palm. I always give her the biggest one I've got, without taking any money, because I don't want her to ever be thin…. One of the sweet things about her is her glasses pressing into her cheeks…It's impossible to see her without giggling, even while she's

showing you her funeral arrangements in complete seriousness!

"I write from right to left on the page."

"Are you Greek? Why don't you use the Latin script?!"

I laugh and think that even though I've worked her for ten months, no one except Ali the vegetable seller knows my name or where I come from! This is the other good thing about this country!

I mean you may take far too long choosing a name for your baby, but at least in the street, you'll say "Hey, are you okay?" to a stranger.

"I'm Iranian, I'm not Greek!"

"Cool, write my name! write down Dana!"

I write from right to left "Dana".

"Wow! So weird…That would make a great tattoo!"

"Aren't Chinese tattoos more popular?" I say humbly.

"I'll think about it, but it's so cool!"

***

He puts his hands either side of my face as if it's an aeroplane, and his hands are landing strips. He opens his eyes, furrowing his neat, wide eyebrows and says: "You should focus on your goal and what you want, move towards it without hesitation!"

He uses the word 'focus' instead of the Persian 'tamarkoz'. He works as an art dealer.

Emmanuel is a kind Italian man, who I call Uncle

_____ My days in London

horned owl, on account of his hairstyle, eyebrows and colouring. I'm sure if I told him this he wouldn't take it as a compliment, but to me he'll always be a friendly horned owl!

He never tastes any of the olives or sweets, but always orders the giant Kalamata, he likes them with the stones in, saying that all the best quality olives should have stones!

I agree with him on the Kalamata at least.

I get a big dish of these teal-purple olives ready.

"Studying early in the morning and working in a kitchen doesn't leave much time for making your film", I say.

"Exactly. But my work is related to Art now, and I came to London 30 years ago! There was no internet or much technology, so you couldn't collaborate with people the other side of the world, or watch whatever you wanted. I chose to work in a restaurant, not be a penniless artist like my friends! If I ever need to work in a kitchen again, I will, but even then I'll focus on my goal. You're right, I studied film and I supposed my work is an imaginary art form, but I don't regret it because I love art in all its forms. Now that you sell olives, you should enjoy it, but focus on your goal too", he says.

"Dear Emmanuel, I'm stuck at a certain point... there's a word in Persian, but I don't know what it is in English. Um...."

I try to explain the Persian word 'gerdab' to him.
"Oh, whirlpool you mean…. So?"
"I mean I knew what my goal was before, but I fell into this whirlpool, and now I'm searching for a stick or something to pull myself out and work towards it again…"
"See, you're a smart guy but easily led!" he laughs.
"Take it easy, Emmanuel!" I laugh.
"You too!"
He's about to take out his phone to show me photos of his new work that's ready to sell, but a customer turns up and stands in front of the olives, staring at me.
"Tomorrow is my day off! What do you think, should I buy olive?! I don't know…"
"See, I need money and you need olives…so let's collaborate!" I laugh.
"Okay, just a few!" he laughs.
"I'm off now…but I'll come and visit you again. Take care…" Emmanuel says.

***

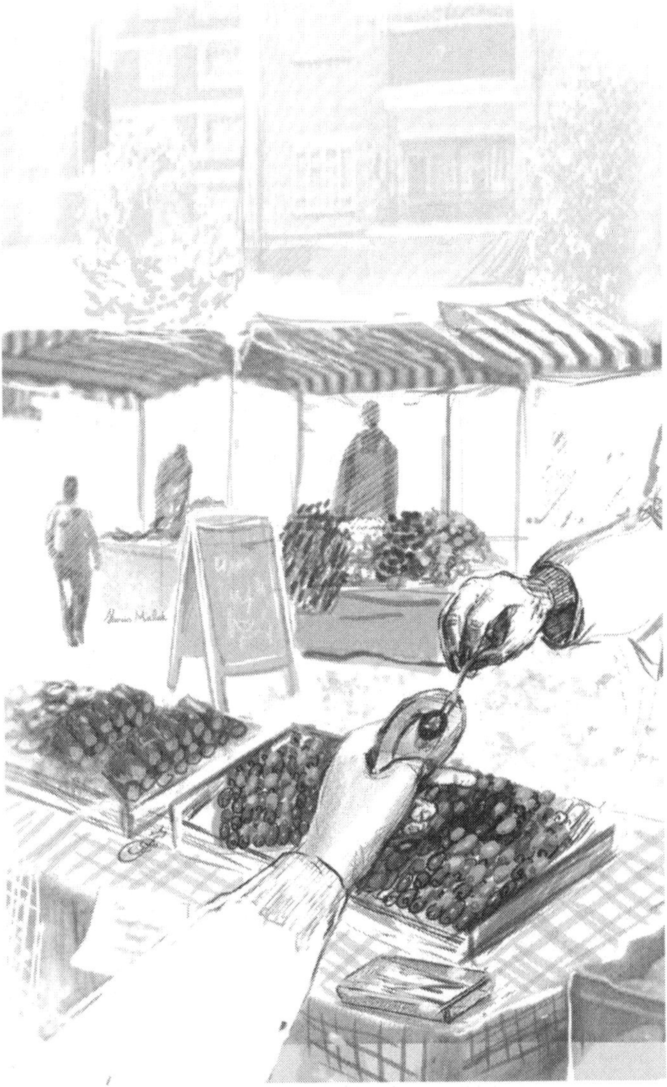

"Oh, hi Raymond!"

"Hi…. Hi…how are you doing? I've come to buy from you for the very last time!"

"Why for the last time?!"

"I've finished my contract with this company".

"I didn't realise you were a contractor! Are you looking for work now?"

"Contract work for oil companies is better than being an employee. Your work is temporary but it's well paid, and has good prospects. I might go to the UAE, I've had a great offer."

I don't know why I feel sad that it's the last time I'll see him. I know that maybe I'll miss the way he speaks Persian, the way he pays me ten pounds, and says seven syllables: mi-bi-na-met, kho-da-fez. "See you later, bye!"

"I'll have my usual, please".

I give him one dish of olives, two pistachio sweets, and a baklava. He gives me his e-mail, and writes his name above it in Persian: ریموند

"I'll email you for sure, I'm going to miss you…"

"All my previous Iranian colleagues said that, but never did. Anyway, I still like them…"

I laugh.

"Ok, I won't promise but I'll try. I'll still be here, whenever you're back in London, come and visit me".

"Sure, you never taught me Persian!!…Have a nice day".

"You too, take care".

* * *

A scrawny young guy says "These sweets look delicious! But I don't eat them at normal times, only when I smoke weed this is what I really want!"

I see he's wearing a short black apron around his waist, the kind that waiters use to keep their notebook and pen in for taking orders.

"Do you work round here? I've never seen you before!"

"I just started a few days ago. I work over there".

He points to one of the cafes and says "You know what? I'm going to be a Policeman next year. I'm going to work everywhere else I can until then…"

"Really? I actually can't imagine you in Police uniform!"

"Yes, my mum and dad always laugh about it too! When I was a kid, I told them I was going to go to England to be a police officer when I grew up!" he laughs.

I wonder why can't you be a Policeman in your own country? What is it that English Police officers can't do that they should be trained for?!

"Are you in your last year of training, then?" I ask.

I was thinking that at this standard, three quarters of British people could join the Police and earn good wages! Maybe he's planning to start next year!

"I left home when I was just eighteen!"

"What makes you think you can join the Police?"

"Because I'm cautious and I'm not scared of anything!"

I want to tell him that being a Police officer requires anything but those particular skills!

"Think about it! I smoke weed myself, and I want to join the Police!" he continues while laughing.

"Really? and they won't notice this?"

"It's fine! how would they find out?"

***

Michael zig-zags towards me from the other end of the market, drunk.
"Have you got a spare cigarette?!"
"No I don't!"
I avoid his eyes and carry on writing.
"I'm not asking for money; I just want a cigarette. I know you've got some…are you Jewish? You want to keep everything for yourself and nothing for anyone else…" he yells.
I ignore him; he's made me very mad, and I'd love to smash his face in rather than get involved, but I know it's because he's a drunkard. I could knock him out with my fist, he'd hit the ground and break something, and then his family might think about helping him!

"Damn it".

Maybe this is a mistake. This isn't Iran! By ignoring him, I'll make him think I'm scared of him!

"Stop it Michael, get out of my face!"

He spits on the ground with contempt, looks round, the goes for an empty fruit crate that David has left after closing. He gets one and comes towards me.

I'm planning to get the box and push him away, say get away from here, kiddo, but the burger seller from down the market comes rushing for him, and they're fighting like two cats.

"Apologise, come on!"

Michael plays innocent and offers me his hand, looks me in the eye and says sorry, but I don't accept it.

"Damn it, why are you even here?!" I say to myself.

***

"That was all your fault", A woman says.

She wags her finger at me as if to tell me off, laughing!

Behind her a handsome Indian man with a bronze tan, black hair and a neat beard laughs and carries on:

"It's the fifth time this week!"

I laugh.

"The usual for you?"

They come here every week to buy a dish of the mammoth sized olives stuffed with Piri piri. One time, she tells me that her husband is addicted to Martini and whenever he gets in from work, he has to have one, but after eating these Peppery olives he never drinks, because of what he calls "The kick of the pepper!"

"This week we'll have two packs!"

I give the olives to the woman and take the money from the man.

"We're going to Brighton next week, so we'll see you in a fortnight…"

"Have a nice week…"

* * *

One of the December nights I was working in Manchester, there was a European Christmas market, and I wanted to stay till the end of the month selling Baklava. But because I'd argued with the manager over the phone, I had to come back to London so I missed the market completely. Now that I think about it, the argument was because I was exhausted from the travelling and my bohemian lifestyle, but I was also upset because I got a ten pound pay cut... they argued that because I was there every day, I would make good money by the end, so therefore they were decreasing my wages by ten pounds a day! I told them "I don't want to work for a company that lowers my wages to increase profit!" Even after they agreed not to dock my wages, I didn't go back, and I was forced to go back to pizza delivery after three years; it made me wonder why I was back in this position again? Lower wages, an employer breathing down my neck, sweeping floors and washing dishes…That made me decide to work for myself from then on.

Michael lumbers towards my booth.

"Excuse me, have you got a spare cigarette?"

"No", I say.

"Sorry…sorry for asking!"

He turns right, then left, lumbering off along the path…

Peter yells "It's time to home, Michael!", and shakes his head.

Michael murmurs over and over "Yes, I know, I know, I know…"

He lumbers off down the path.

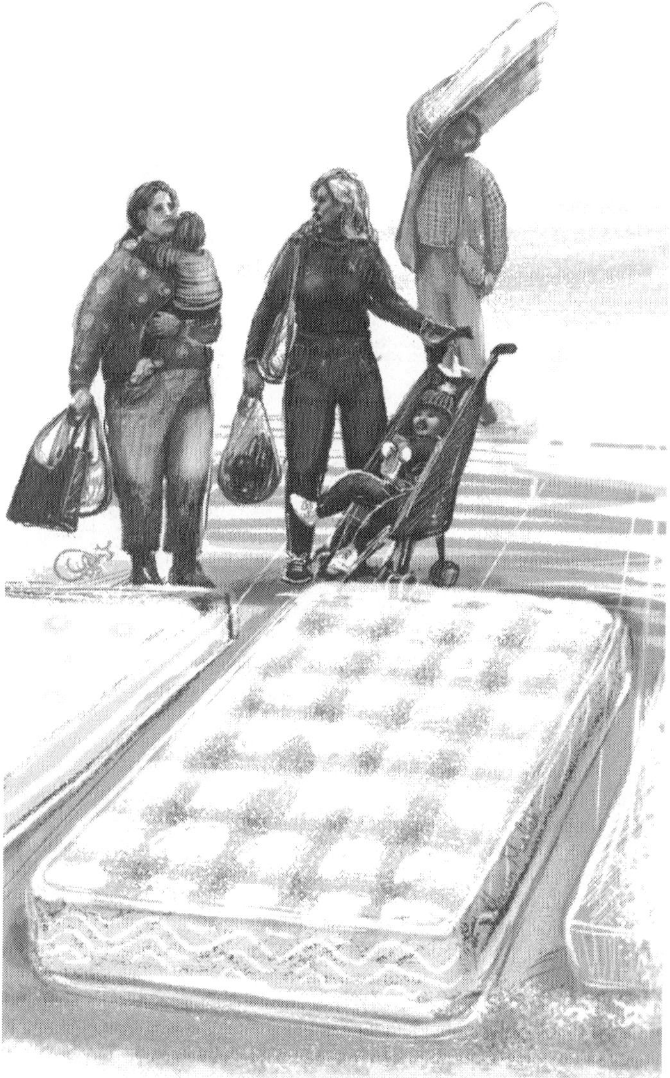

Abraham passes between my stall and Peter's in his huge, knackered white van, getting as close as ten centimeters from me. His foot on the pedal, he fills the whole path with gas fumes, only stopping between his own stall and Leo's, despite all the sellers' nagging...

"Do you want to shred our nerves, Abraham?" Leo yells.

Abraham gets out of the van clumsily, because of his great height, and looks at Leo with a smile as if to say "Take it easy, man!"

His loose navy overcoat falls onto his faded jeans, and he moves the gray hat he always wears. It's a relief to see his head get some fresh air!

He goes to the back of the van, and it's obvious the lock is broken!

He borrows one of the locks from the garage door to use, while heaving a mattress onto his shoulder...

Leo speaks to him so loudly I can hear them from five booths down.

"Abraham, do you know why you get on my nerves, apart from the fact that you come and go earlier than everyone else??

Abraham puts the mattress in his van, and says "You can tell me if you want to!"

"Because you're black!"

I try and see Abraham's reaction. The huge, unwieldy mattress is light as cotton on his shoulders; I see his white teeth and smile…he raises his eyebrows and widens his eyes and says "No…No…don't ever be such a racist again…by the way, I'm not black, and I'm brown!"

He laughs with his whole spirit, and it's clear from his dignified answer that Leo's attempt to enrage him is useless. Then he just murmurs something to himself I can't hear.

He puts three sizes of mattress on his shoulders – single, double and king size. Every day he puts them on the ground and calls it his display cabinet! Whenever someone stands in front of them chatting, he appears suddenly from behind them, glowering. He won't smile, and he intimidates them menacingly, saying don't stand in the way of my shop window, please!

Whenever he comes here, and I ask him how it's going today, he answers, "Who knows? Our job is a gamble, some days you earn just five pounds, other days you get a months' money in a single day!"

If anyone mistakenly guesses that he's Jamaican, he loves to tell them "I'm from the Dominican Republic", puffing up with pride!

After packing up, when everyone wants him to move his van, he says "You know, this van is so old it will hardly start! I need some stuff from the supermarket, let me come back and start it after that!"

His van always takes a few goes before it starts…

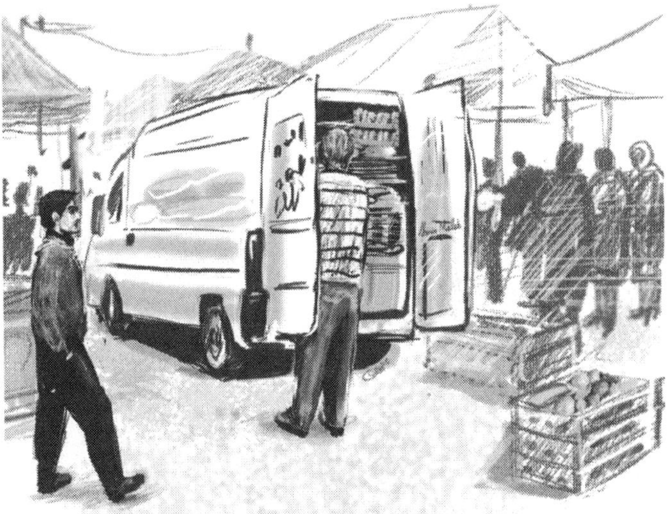

He's like a rapper. Wearing a big hat and long black top with an unusual print on it, and a long gold chain hanging down past his belly. He's carrying heavy bags and he's going blue, but he has an open child-like face…

"You really want to buy olives with your hands full?!"
"My wife is at home. She said dinner's ready and to be home soon, and I thought I can't go back empty handed; but she always complains about whatever I bring!"
"It sounds like you should be happy your dinner's ready…but apparently that's not enough, why not?"
"This is what it's like with an older partner! It makes no difference if the older one is a man or a woman! Tell me, what kind of Chili olives have you got?"

I point to three types that are stuffed: one with green jalapeno peppers, one with red Piri-piri peppers and one soaked in Harissa sauce.

"Give me a packet with all three mixed together".

"How old do you think I am?" he puts the packet on the ground.

"I'm not good a guessing ages, but I'd say between twenty-eight and thirty-two?!"

"Look, I'm forty-two!" he closes his eyes tightly and smiles.

"Really?! But you said your wife is older! Which means…"

"Yes, I'm pretty senior myself, but she…" he thinks a little and says "She's fifty-three…You see? Even at my age, there's someone to criticize and nag you!"

I put the rest of the olives he ordered in a packet and give it to him.

He puts it on the ground beside the others and gives me twenty pounds.

"How many years have you lived together?"

"Oh, it's nearly eleven years!"

"So I bet with all those memories, getting divorced would not be easy!" I give him his change.

"You know what? There's a reason I could never leave her, I renovated every part of our house, it's so modern and easy…I'm so attached to it! And once you let one thing go, it's like dominoes…you know what I mean?! I'm comfortable, that's all…"

"Being comfortable is important, but it's not everything!" I say.
"Are you single?"
"Yes, but I don't think I'll ever share my home with anyone ever! For obvious reasons!"
"You never know; it could happen more than once! That's life, dude…" he laughs loudly.
I laugh.
"I should get a taxi". He looks at his shopping. "Great to meet you". He shakes my hand.
"There's a mini cab over the road there. Great to meet you too!"
"Take it easy!" he says.
I want to tell him he's the one who should take it easy, but instead I say "Okay, have a nice day!"
"Yes, my dinner's ready!" he answers, still laughing.

* * *

I look at the time, it's quarter to five.
"I'll pack up in fifteen minutes…" I tell myself.
I feel like my mind is too tired to think…I should forget about Alexander Palace, and I should go to Baskin Robbins to eat cotton candy ice cream on my way home!
If I get there just before seven, then stay till I feel like going home, I'll throw myself onto my bed, with my shoes still on, maybe I'll just have time to brush my teeth.
Yes…I like eating these red and blue cotton candy ice creams, they remind me of my childhood…not because I liked ice cream as a child, or even that I had a good life in my childhood, no…! It's because

the idea of childhood evokes a sense of ease, of not having responsibilities or mental stress...

I need a reason to eat ice cream...usually it's to celebrate something...for example, starting a new job, a sunny day off, a new plan or even celebrating a big decision.

I can't justify buying cotton candy ice cream for no reason!

"Mmmm, ahhh.... for finishing a day's work!"

It makes me laugh.

I think no one but me could persuade myself I deserve a red and blue cotton candy ice cream!

I take the money from the till, count it and put it in my pocket. With my gloves on, I put the olives in the bucket under the table.

I think after cleaning the dishes, I should park the van beside my stall, and maybe someone will buy some sweets for tonight's pudding, and I'll earn my ice cream money.

Just thinking about ice cream fills me with energy.

"Lets focus on cotton candy ice cream..." I think.

—×—
F
M

© Firouz Media 2022

Made in the USA
Columbia, SC
30 May 2022